Crainquebille

ILLUSTRATED BY BERNARD LAMOTTE

Crainquebille

[L'AFFAIRE CRAINQUEBILLE] BY ANATOLE
FRANCE: NEWLY TRANSLATED, WITH AN
INTRODUCTION, BY JACQUES LeCLERCQ
AND ILLUSTRATED BY BERNARD LAMOTTE

The Heritage Press, New York

Introduction

FOUR generations of readers appreciated the works of Anatole France during his lifetime (1844-1924). In other words, men born in 1800 might have saluted his brilliant early work in their eighties and those born in 1900 were in their twenties when he died. He was born the same year as Verlaine, four years after Zola, six years before de Maupassant and ten years before Rimbaud. To the last two generations of the century, he was a veritable idol. The majority of its members appreciated in him the philosopher amused by the idiosyncrasies of life (no great thinker, he, but he provoked thought); the scholar (highly erudite in the most unexpected and recondite fields); the artist (a colorist in his depiction of background and characters as well as in his inimitable prose style); the dilettante of suave and exquisite taste; and the humanitarian.

Our own century has been less kind. Amid the ebullience of the twenties, the anxiety of the thirties, the agonies and ardors of World War II, and our own present disquiet, what place for a man and writer of his stamp? Already his funeral was the signal for shameful manifestations in the street and his successor at the French Academy insulted the dead master by forbearing from pronouncing his name in the eulogy each academician-elect makes of his predecessor. The huge sales of his books began to dwindle. On a different plane one is minded of Père Crainquebille who worked bravely for a half-century only to suffer a fall from grace.

The literary reasons for this are readily recognizable. He was always an individualist, a solitary. And, in the main, the twenties were a period of movements, conscious or unconscious. There were the war novels... Proust and Proustism... Dadaism and Surréalism... cosmopolitanism and exoticism... the new impetus given to the regional novel... the later naturalism (for naturalism was not dead, as people had thought)... and the increased vogue of foreign authors in French translation.

The more material reasons, too, were quite clear. As a disciple of Renan, Anatole France could not but be a sceptic in religion and everything else which embodied the highest ideals of a vast number of people. As the third of the great trinity of writers who best illustrated Gallic wit — Rabelais and Voltaire are the other two — he was bound to give offense. Specifically, this man who loved old rare books, old works of art and his old slippers, was never loath, despite his seeming gentleness, to descend into the arena of politics and espouse a cause he believed to be just. Now most of these causes lay towards the Left, and increasingly so as he grew older.

Georg Brandes, the Danish critic, has left us a description of Anatole France addressing a Socialist Congress in the early 1900's. He read his paper, his delivery was poor, but the irony and the style of his text were exactly the sort of thing we find in Part IV of *Crainquebille*. And he had greater assets to offer his party: his world reputation and his brilliant pen. Obviously he acquired the enmity of the Right and even of one part of the Center, for politics is scarcely the calm and deliberate pursuit that literature was for the sage who wrote *Monsieur Bergeret* and *Penguin Island*. It is inappropriate to go into the question here, but it may surely be said that, had there been more Frenchmen of the same mind and heart as Anatole

France, then Marshal Pétain and those of his ideology would have found fewer supporters and sympathizers.

Crainquebille, written in 1901 when its author was fifty-six years old, offers a splendid example of his championship of a just cause, for the whole work is inspired by the Dreyfus Case and abounds in references to it. It is in a sense a parable. Our dilettante in this case was on the right side which was, as I have said, the Left. Men fight as they can; the best fighter seizes the weapon best adapted to his mode of fighting. Zola's was an impassioned and utterly fearless indignation, Clemenceau's a mordant ferocity, Anatole France's that "irony and pity" which I dare call his slogan, which has been much mocked since by lesser men, and which more than once stood the cause of justice in good stead. His plea for everything that is noble and honest and self-respecting and human against everything the Government represented was the more stirring because of the pessimistic note it struck in *Crainquebille*.

Many people think *Crainquebille* its creator's masterpiece. There is much to be said for this view. Inspired by a contemporary political outrage, it seems more immediate than other works where allusion plays a greater part. We have its author in it in the person of Monsieur Jean Lermite, the etcher, who presents the Apologia for Monsieur le Président, just as we have him in other books under the names of Sylvestre Bonnard, Dr. Trublet, Jérôme Coignard, Monsieur Bergeret, *etc.* We have a wonderful realism of setting with the Paris of the Court and the Paris of the streets, small stores, markets, wineshops, garrets, and doubtless, at the bitter end of the road, the Seine to bring deliverance. We have a wonderful realism of character with judges, lawyers, court officials, various types of policemen, one artist, one physician, shopkeepers, hawkers, one prostitute and our immortal hero. We have a wonderful realism of dialogue which makes the translator's labor of love a labor of Hercules — or should I say Sisyphus? And we have lines, nay, passages which could be culled from the story and plastered over the walls of our own schools and courthouses to high advantage.

The end of the story — an example of the author's flawless artistry — has Crainquebille plunging into the rain and the darkness. To the reader who knew the Paris of that time there is but one conclusion: he is headed for the river, which solved the problems of so many of his class and indeed of other classes.

Thus, for all our smiles and chuckles at the irony of the beginning, we heave a sigh of compassion for the pity of the end.

JACQUES LE CLERCQ

Crainquebille

BY ANATOLE FRANCE

I

By way of introduction

JUSTICE in all its majesty is inherent in each and every sentence pronounced by a Judge in the name of the Sovereign People. A pushcart pedlar called Jérôme Crainquebille was destined to learn how august The Law can be when he found himself arraigned in the Paris Police Court, charged with uttering gross and abusive insults against an Officer of the Force in the discharge of his duty.

Having entered the awesome, sombre courtroom, he was placed upon the bench reserved for accused persons. From this point of vantage, he surveyed the three Judges, the Clerks of the Court, the Attorneys in their medieval robes, the Usher wearing his rich Chain of Office, and, over a partition, the bared heads of the spectators. He surveyed himself, too, on the lofty seat he occupied; it was as if a mere appearance before magistrates conferred an ominous honor upon accused persons.

At the rear of the courtroom, Monsieur le Président Bourriche, the Presiding Judge, throned it over the two Assistant Judges, one at his right, the other at his left. The Presiding Judge wore, over his bosom, the insignia of the Palmes Académiques — the palm leaves of a minor decoration usually awarded for distinction in some intellectual pursuit.

A bust, symbolizing the Republic, and a Christ on the Cross, were affixed over the Judicial Bench. Thus to Crainquebille it seemed that all laws, human and divine, loomed in suspense over his wretched head. Obviously this filled him with a righteous terror. For he was not of a philosophical turn of mind. He did not puzzle over what this bust and this crucifix might mean, nor did he seek to ascertain whether Jesus (symbol of Christianity) and Marianne (symbol of the Third French Republic) found themselves in harmony within a Court at Law. Yet this question was one worthy of some reflection.

Are not Papal Doctrine and Canon Law at considerable

variance upon many points with the Constitution of the French Republic and the *Code Civil?* More, the Decretals (that voluminous collection of legal decisions accumulated under a succession of Popes) have not been abolished — or, if they have, no one has yet been informed of the fact.

Further, the French Republic still maintains that it is in no wise dependent upon the powers of the Pontiff.

Crainquebille might therefore have declared to his judges with some reason:

"Gentlemen Magistrates! As Monsieur Emile Loubet, President of the French Republic, has never been anointed, this Christ, looming above your heads, challenges your authority by virtue of the Councils of Papal and Catholic episcopacy, whose canons are supreme to the faithful. Either He hangs here to remind you of the rights of the Church and thus nullifies *your* rights, or His presence is senseless."

To which Monsieur le Président Bourriche, Presiding Judge, might well have replied:

"The Court would inform the accused, Crainquebille, that the Kings of France have always been at outs with the Pope. Guillaume de Nogaret, Chancellor of France under King Philip the Fair in the Thirteenth Century, was duly excommunicated; but he did not allow so paltry a factor to drive him

out of office. This Christ you see over the Judicial Bench is
not the Christ of Pope Gregory VII who humiliated the Emperor in the Eleventh Century, nor again the Christ of Pope
Boniface VIII who bitterly opposed our own King Philip,
previously mentioned, in the Thirteenth. This Christ above
my head is, if you will, the Christ of the Gospels Who knew
never one word of Canon Law and never heard one human
being mention the Holy Decretals."

Crainquebille, in turn, might permissibly have countered:

"The Christ of the Gospels was a violent agitator. What is
more, He has been the victim of a sentence which for nine-
teen hundred years has been considered by all the peoples of
Christendom to be a capital miscarriage of justice. I defy the
Court—in the persons of you, Monsieur le Président and your
Assessors — to sentence me in His name to so much as forty-
eight hours in jail."

But Crainquebille indulged in no historical, political or social considerations. He was lost in the deepest astonishment.
The pomp and circumstance into which he had been so suddenly projected impressed him with a high notion of justice.
Filled with awe and beside himself with terror, he was wil-
ling to depute to his judges all question of his innocence or
guilt. In his own conscience, he did not believe himself to be

a criminal. But then how paltry the conscience of a pushcart pedlar when pitted against the symbols of the law and the ministers of social prosecution! Already his lawyer had half-persuaded him that he was not innocent.

A preliminary investigation, conducted in great haste, revealed the charges that weighed upon him.

II

Of the misadventure that befell Crainquebille

Jérôme Crainquebille, a hawker of vegetables, roamed over the city of Paris, wheeling his pushcart and bawling: "Cabbages! Turnips! Carrots! Buy my cabbages! turnips! carrots!" And when he had leeks he would cry: "Asparagus — in bundles!" because leeks are the poor man's asparagus.

Now on October 20, at noon, he happened to be making his way down the Rue Montmartre when Madame Bayard,

the shoemaker's wife, emerged from her small shop, and, approaching the leguminous vehicle, picked up a bunch of leeks disparagingly:

"Don't look fresh to me, those leeks!" she opined. "How much a bunch?"

"Fifteen *sous*, Madame Bayard, ma'ame. None better in the markets!"

"Fifteen *sous* for three wretched leeks?" she demanded indignantly. And, with a gesture of disgust, she tossed the leeks back onto the pushcart.

At precisely this moment, Police Officer 64 appeared on the scene.

"Move on!" he told Crainquebille.

Now for over a half-century Crainquebille had been "moving on" from early morning to dewy eve; to receive such an order seemed to him legitimate and in agreement with the natural course of events; and he was perfectly disposed to obey. So he urged Madame Bayard to choose whatever he had that she fancied.

"So I'm to wade through your rotten leeks to find a good bunch?" she said sourly. And once again she fingered each bunch individually. Then, choosing the one she considered the finest, she hugged it to her, much as, in church paintings, martyred lady-saints clasp the palm of victory to their bosoms.

"It's fourteen *sous* I'll give you and not a *centime* more! That's plenty! You'll have to wait, too. I've no cash on me; I must go back to the shop!"

Holding the leeks fast in her embrace, she moved off, close on the heels of a woman customer who had entered the shoe-store carrying a baby.

Then, for the second time, Officer 64 said to Crainquebille: "Move on, there!"

"But I'm waiting for my money!"

"I'm not asking you to wait for your money," the policeman replied firmly, "I'm telling you to move on!"

In her shoestore Madame Bayard was busy trying a pair of blue shoes on the feet of a baby eighteen months old. The infant's mother was in a great hurry. Meanwhile the green heads of the leeks lay forgotten on the counter.

During the fifty or more years that Crainquebille had been propelling his pushcart through the streets, he had learned to obey the representatives of authority. This time, however, he was caught in a peculiar position, between the Scylla of a duty and the Charybdis of a right. He did not understand that enjoyment of an individual right in no wise excused him from performance of a social duty. Too much he stressed his private right to receive the fourteen *sous* that were his due; too little his public duty which was to wheel his pushcart before him and to move on and on and on for evermore.

As Crainquebille stood his ground, Officer 64, coolly and collectedly and for the third time, ordered Crainquebille to move on. Unlike Officer Montauciel, whose habit it was constantly to threaten but never to act sternly, Officer 64 was sparing in admonishment but very prompt to punitive action. Such was his character. Although a whit sly, he was an excellent public servant and a loyal soldier. Combining the courage of a lion with the gentleness of a child, he knew nothing beyond the regulations governing his official duties.

"Didn't you hear me? I told you to move on!"

Now Crainquebille's reason for standing pat was too weighty, in his opinion, for him not to deem it sufficient. He explained simply and artlessly:

"God's truth, didn't I tell you I was waiting for my money?"

Officer 64 merely replied:

"Do you want me to run you in for violating police regulations? If that's what you want, just say so!"

At these words, Crainquebille slowly shrugged his shoulders, looked tragically at the policeman, then raised his eyes to heaven in a glance that said:

"God be my witness, am I a contemner of laws? Do I play fast and loose with the rules and ordinances which govern my ambulatory calling? At five this morning I was on the floor of the market of Les Halles. Since seven o'clock I've been trundling my pushcart, bruising and blistering my hands on its shafts and crying: 'Cabbages! Turnips! Carrots!' I'm over sixty, yes, over sixty! I'm worn out! And you ask me am I raising the black banner of rebellion? You're making fun of me and your jest is a cruel one!"

Either the expression of Crainquebille's glance escaped the officer or he found in it no excuse for disobedience; at any rate, he inquired curtly and roughly whether Crainquebille understood him.

At this precise moment, the traffic jam in the Rue Montmartre became acute. Cabs, drays, carts, busses, trucks, blocking one another, seemed inextricably tangled and welded together. Shouts and oaths soared above the quivering immobility of this sea of vehicles. Across far distances and with studious deliberation, cabmen and butchers' boys exchanged heroic insults, and the bus-conductors, regarding Crainquebille as the cause of all this confusion, denounced him as a "*Sale Poireau!*" which means both "Dirty Leek!" and "Fool and Imbecile!"

Meanwhile, on the sidewalk, the curious thronged about

Crainquebille and the policeman to enjoy the dispute. And the policeman, finding himself the focal point of all these eyes, had no further thought but to display his authority.

"All right, you asked for it!" he said, drawing a filthy note-book and the stump of a pencil from his pocket.

Crainquebille, obedient to some inner force, steadfastly pursued his original idea. Besides, by now it was impossible for him either to advance or to retreat. The wheel of his pushcart was unhappily caught in the wheel of a milkman's cart. Tearing at his hair through his cap:

"But I told you... I told you..." he cried, "I'm waiting for my money.... There's a fine thing for you! *Misère de misère*, God help us! *Bon sang de bon sang*, God's truth, damn it!"

Though these words expressed despair rather than rebellion, Officer 64 considered that he had been insulted. To him, of course, any insult naturally took on the traditional, regular, consecrated, and so to speak, liturgical form. This form is invariably the cry *"Mort aux Vaches!"*, an untranslatable Gallicism which implies in its three words that the police are swine, spies, idlers, grafters and stoolpigeons and that death is too good for them. Thus the relatively wild words of the delinquent were gathered and made concrete in the policeman's ears in this grossly abusive idiom.

"You said '*Mort aux Vaches!*', eh? All right! *You* come along with *me!*"

Crainquebille, in excess of stupor and distress, gazed at Officer 64 from out of great sun-bleared eyes. Crossing his arms over his blue blouse, in a cracked voice emerging now from the top of his head, now from under his heels, he cried:

"*I said 'Mort aux Vaches!'* . . . ? *I* said that? Oh!"

Crainquebille's arrest aroused a salvo of laughter from the tradesmen and errand boys who watched it, for it gratified the taste all crowds entertain for violent and ignoble spectacles. Suddenly an old man thrust his way through the throng — a man with a sad face, clad in black, and wearing a high hat. Going up to the policeman:

"You are mistaken, Officer," he observed very gently and very firmly in a low voice. "This man did not insult you."

"You mind your own business," the policeman replied curtly. But he did not threaten because he was addressing a well-dressed man.

The old man insisted very calmly and very tenaciously, at which the officer enjoined him to argue the point at the Station House.

Meanwhile Crainquebille was crying out:

"So I said *'Mort aux Vaches!'* . . . I said that . . . Oh!"

As he was voicing his amazement, Madame Bayard, the shoemaker's wife, emerged from her shop with fourteen *sous* in her hand. But Officer 64 already had Crainquebille by the scruff of the neck, and Madame Bayard, believing that nothing is due to a man who is being led off to the police station, returned the fourteen *sous* to her apron pocket.

Then, suddenly seeing his pushcart impounded, his freedom lost, an abyss yawning at his feet, and the sun blotted out from the skies, Crainquebille murmured:

"Good Lord! Who would have thought it?"

Appearing before the Police Captain, the old gentleman declared that he had been held up by the traffic jam and had thus witnessed the whole scene. He insisted that the officer had not been insulted, indeed that he had been utterly mistaken. He identified himself as Dr. David Matthieu, Chief Physician at the Ambroise Paré Hospital and Officer of the Legion of Honor.

At any other period of history, such testimony would have enlightened the Police Captain sufficiently. But in France in 1900 intellectuals were suspect.

Crainquebille's arrest was maintained: he spent that night in the prison and was transferred next morning in the Black Maria to the Police Court.

Prison did not seem to him either painful or humiliating, but, rather, a necessity. What struck him on entering was the cleanliness of the walls and of the stone floor.

"Whew!" he exclaimed. "For a clean place, this is a clean place! God's truth, you could eat off the floor!"

When he was left alone, he tried to draw out a stool to sit

on but noticed that it was fastened to the wall. He gave loud vent to his surprise:

"There's a funny idea!" he said. "God's truth, there's a thing I'd never have dreamed of, I'm sure!"

Having sat down, he twiddled his thumbs and remained lost in astoundment. The silence and the solitude overwhelmed him. He was lonely and bored and he worried about his pushcart, impounded with its load of cabbages, carrots, celery, lamb's-lettuce, corn-salad and dandelion. Anxiously he wondered:

"Where have they clapped away my pushcart?"

On the third day, he received a visit from his lawyer, Maître Lemerle, one of the youngest members of the Paris Bar and President of a section of the Ligue de la Patrie Française, an organization devoted to the championship of Church and Army and to the persecution of Captain Dreyfus.

Crainquebille attempted to tell his lawyer the whole story, which proved to be no easy matter, unaccustomed as he was to conversation. Yet with a little help, he might perhaps have managed. But at every word Crainquebille uttered, the lawyer shook his head doubtfully, and, turning over his papers:

"Hum, hmmm!" he murmured. "I can see nothing about all this in the report. . . ."

Then, twirling his blond mustache with an uninterested air, he added:

"For your own good, it would perhaps be preferable for you to plead guilty. For my part, I consider your system of whole-sale denial to be extraordinarily unwise."

And from that moment onward, Crainquebille would cheerfully have made confession, had he but known what to confess.

III

Of Crainquebille at the bar of justice

Monsieur le Président
Bourriche, Presiding Judge, devoted six whole minutes to
questioning Crainquebille. This examination might have
proved more enlightening had the accused replied to the
questions asked of him. But Crainquebille was not accus-
tomed to discussion; besides, in such exalted company, a sense of

21

awe and fear sealed his lips. So he was silent and the Presiding Judge himself answered his own questions. These vicarious replies were damning. Monsieur le Président concluded:

"In brief, you admit you said '*Mort aux Vaches!*'"

"I said '*Mort aux Vaches!*' because the officer said '*Mort aux Vaches!*' So then I said '*Mort aux Vaches!*' too."

He sought to make the Court understand that, bowled over by the most unexpected of accusations, in his consternation he had merely repeated the strange words which were falsely attributed to him and which he had certainly never uttered. He had said "*Mort aux Vaches!*" as he might have said: "I? Why, I *couldn't* insult anyone. How could you believe it?"

But Monsieur le Président Bourriche, Presiding Judge, saw things in a very different light.

"Do you mean to say," he challenged, "that it was the policeman himself who first uttered this exclamation?"

Crainquebille gave up trying to explain. It was too difficult.

"You do not persist in your denial," Monsieur le Président told Crainquebille. "And you are right!"

Then he had the witnesses called before the Court.

Officer 64, Bastien Matra by name, swore to speak the truth, the whole truth and nothing but the truth. Then he testified as follows:

"I was on my beat on October 20 at noon when, going down the Rue Montmartre I noticed a person who appeared to be a hawker and who was improperly stationing his push-cart opposite Number 328 Rue Montmartre, thus blocking the traffic all the way down the line. Three times, no less, I ordered him to move on; but he refused to comply with my orders. I then warned him that I was about to charge him. His reply was to shout: *'Mort aux Vaches!'* This seemed to me to be insulting — being gross and abusive language — so I arrested him."

The three magistrates listened to this firm, responsible testimony with evident favor. The defense had subpoenaed Madame Bayard, proprietress of a shoemaker's shop, and Monsieur David Matthieu, Chief Physician at the Ambroise Paré Hospital, Officer of the Legion of Honor. Madame Bayard stated that she had seen or heard nothing. Dr. Matthieu testified that he was in the midst of a throng assembled around the policeman who was ordering the pedlar to move on. His testimony occasioned an incident in the Court.

"I was present at the scene," he declared. "I noticed that the officer was mistaken; he had not been insulted. I went up to him and told him so. The officer insisted upon keeping the pedlar under arrest and invited me to follow him to the Police

Station. I did this. Appearing before the Police Captain, I repeated what I had told the officer."

"You may be seated," said the Presiding Judge. "Call back the witness Matra."

Matra took the stand. The Presiding Judge continued:

"Matra, when you proceeded to arrest the accused, did Dr. Matthieu point out to you that you were committing an error?"

"The fact is, Monsieur le Président, he insulted me."

"What did he say to you?"

"He said '*Mort aux Vaches!*'"

A buzz of comment and roars of laughter arose from the public.

"You may withdraw," said the Presiding Judge hastily. And he warned the public that if such unbecoming behavior occurred once more, he would clear the courtroom. Meanwhile Defense Counsel was waving the sleeves of his robe triumphantly and at this juncture everyone believed that Crainquebille would be acquitted.

Calm having been restored, Maître Lemerle rose to defend Crainquebille. He began his plea by praising the officers of the Police Force.

"Here are modest servants of the social system, who, for a

ridiculously low salary, endure tremendous fatigue, face constant danger, and practise a daily heroism. They are former soldiers who have remained soldiers. Soldiers — the word expresses all ...."

Next, effortlessly, Maître Lemerle rose to very lofty considerations about military virtues in the abstract. He declared himself one of those who "will not allow anyone to impugn this national army to which I am proud to belong."

The Presiding Judge nodded in agreement.

In point of fact, Maître Lemerle was a lieutenant in the reserve. He was also a candidate of the Nationalist Party, supporting Church, State and Army, in the old quarter of Les Vieilles Hudrettes, named for Hudry who established a foundling home there in the Twelfth Century.

The attorney continued:

"No, indeed, I do not fail to appreciate the unassuming and valuable services rendered daily to the valiant population of Paris by these wardens of the peace. Nor would I have consented to defend Crainquebille, gentlemen, if I saw in him one who had insulted a former soldier. My client is accused of having said *'Mort aux Vaches!'* The meaning of this phrase is perfectly clear. If you consult *Le Dictionnaire de la Langue Verte,* that lexicon of slang and cant, you will find, — and I quote: '*Vachard*, a loafer, a good-for-nothing, a gawk, one who stretches himself out lazily like a cow instead of working.' There is also the term '*Vache*,' referring to a spy, a stool pigeon, one who sells himself to the police. In certain strata of society, '*Mort aux Vaches!*' is a current term. But the whole question rests upon this: How did Crainquebille say it? Indeed, did he actually say it? Permit me, gentlemen, to doubt it!

"I do not suspect Officer 64, Officer Matra, of the slightest evil intent. But, as we have said, he accomplishes an arduous and laborious task. He is often worn out, harassed, under a strain. In such conditions, he may well have been the victim of some sort of aural hallucination. And when he comes to tell you, gentlemen, that Dr. David Matthieu, an Officer of the Legion of Honor, Chief Physician at the Ambroise Paré Hospital, a gentleman, a man of the world, and a prince of science, cried '*Mort aux Vaches!*' then we are forced to recognize that Matra is a prey to an obsession and, if the term is not too harsh, to the mania of persecution.

"And even had Crainquebille cried '*Mort aux Vaches!*' we should still have to prove whether such words on his lips could constitute a misdemeanor. Crainquebille is the natural child of a woman pedlar who was tainted by long years of alcoholism and depravity. Crainquebille was born an alcoholic. Behold him before you, brutalized by sixty years of poverty. Gentlemen, you must conclude that he is irresponsible."

Maître Lemerle sat down. Presently Monsieur le Président Bourriche, the Presiding Judge, muttered a sentence whereby Jérôme Crainquebille was condemned to a fortnight in prison and to a fine of fifty francs. The magistrates convicted him on the strength of the testimony of Officer 64, Bastien Matra.

As he was being led away down the long dark corridors of the sombre Palais de Justice, Crainquebille experienced an immense need of sympathy. So he turned to the soldier who was escorting him — a Municipal Guard — and using the popular abbreviation, called three times:

"'*Cipal!* . . . '*Cipal!* . . . Hey, '*Cipal!*"

And he sighed:

"If anyone had told me just a fortnight ago that this was going to happen to me . . . ."

Then, from the fruit of his meditation:

"Those gentlemen talk too fast. They talk well but they talk too fast. You can't make them understand you. '*Cipal*, don't you think they talk too fast?"

But the soldier walked on straight ahead without answering or turning his head.

Crainquebille asked him:

"Why don't you answer me?"

The soldier kept silent. And Crainquebille said bitterly:

"A man talks to a dog, don't he? Why won't you talk to *me?* You never open your mouth, eh? I know why: it's because you're afraid of the stink that would come out of it."

IV

Apologia for Monsieur le Président Bourriche, the presiding judge

AFTER sentence had been passed, while the Clerk of the Court was calling another case, a few spectators and two or three lawyers left the courtroom. Those who went out did not reflect upon the Crainquebille case for they had found it of little interest and already thought no more about it. One man alone, Monsieur Jean Lermite, an etcher, who had happened to come to the Palais by chance, did meditate upon what he had just heard and seen.

Putting his arm round the shoulders of Maître Joseph Aubarrée, the lawyer, his friend:

"Monsieur le Président Bourriche, the Presiding Judge, is worthy of high praise," said Lermite, "for his ability in avoiding idle mental curiosity and in eschewing that intellectual pride which aspires to know everything. By taking the contradictory testimony of Officer Matra and of Dr. David Matthieu and pitting one against the other, the judge would have followed a course leading only to doubt and uncertainty. The method which consists in submitting facts to critical examination is incompatible with the smooth administration of justice. If a magistrate were so rash as to follow the critical method, his sentences would depend upon his personal sagacity (which is most often limited) and upon human infirmity (which is infinite). What authoritative standards could this method possibly set up? Who shall not say that the historical method is completely unequipped to supply a judge with the certitudes he requires? Sir Walter Raleigh's experience proves this conclusively.

"One day when Sir Walter, a prisoner in the Tower of London, was working as usual on the second part of his *History of the World*, a brawl broke out under his window. Rising, he looked out to watch the various fighters and, when he returned to his work, he believed that he had observed them very accurately. But on the morrow, having discussed this affair with one of his friends, who had been present at the row and had even taken part in it, Sir Walter was flatly contradicted by his friend on every single point. Reflecting then upon the diffi-

culty of ascertaining the truth about events historically remote, when he had been mistaken on what had happened under his very eyes, he tossed the manuscript of his *History* into the fire.

"If judges had the same scruples as Sir Walter Raleigh, they too would consign all their summaries to the flames. But they have no right to do this for they would be denying justice and committing a crime. We must forego learning the truth but must not forego judging prisoners. Those who claim that decisions handed down in Courts of Law should be founded upon a methodical sifting of facts are dangerous sophists and perfidious enemies of justice, both civil and military.

"Monsieur le Président Bourriche has too judicial a mind to allow his sentences to depend upon reason and knowledge, because the conclusions of reason and knowledge are subject to eternal dispute. He founds his sentences upon dogmas and assimilates them to tradition; they are therefore equal in authority to the commandments of the Church. His sentences are canonical; in other words, he derives them from a certain number of sacred canons. Notice, for instance, how he classifies testimony, not according to the uncertain and deceptive factors of likelihood and human truth, but according to certain, intrinsic, permanent, manifest factors. He weighs them, using weapons of war for weights. By this I mean that he classifies them according to their importance, that is according to the influence a witness may exert or the position he may enjoy. Could anything be at once simpler and wiser?

"All notion of a policeman's humanity having been set aside, and this policeman having been conceived metaphysically as a number on the rolls of the police force and according to the categories of the ideal police, our Presiding Judge holds this policeman's evidence to be irrefutable. Not that Bastien Matra, born at Cinto-Monte in Corsica, appears to him incapable of error. He never thought that Bastien Matra was endowed with a striking gift for observation nor that he applied an exact and rigorous method to the examination of facts. Truth to tell, it is not Bastien Matra he is really considering but Officer 64. Every man is fallible, he thinks. Surely Tom, Dick and Harry may be mistaken when the greatest scientists and philosophers of all times and nations — Descartes, Gassendi, Leibnitz, Newton, Bichat and Claude Bernard — were open to error! We all make mistakes and at any moment. The causes of our errors are innumerable. The perceptions of our senses and the judgments of our minds are sources of illusions and grounds for uncertainty. We must not rely on the testimony of a single man: *Testis unus, testis nullus*, said the Romans, or in other words, a single witness is no witness. Who shall prove a case on the testimony of one man only?

"But we can have faith in a Number. Bastien Matra of Cinto-Monte in Corsica is fallible; but Officer 64 (his humanity having been set aside) cannot err. He is an entity. An entity possesses nothing of what dwells in men to disturb, corrupt and abuse them. An entity is pure, unalterable and unmitigated. Accordingly the Court did not hesitate to reject the evidence of Dr. David Matthieu, who is but one man; it preferred to admit that of Officer 64, who is a pure idea, and, as it were, a ray of brightness sent down by God to enlighten the judges.

"By arguing thus, M. le Président Bourriche ensures for himself a kind of infallibility, the only infallibility to which a judge may aspire. When the man who testifies is armed with a sword, the sword must be hearkened to, not the man. The man is contemptible and may be wrong; the sword is not contemptible and is always right. The Presiding Judge has read deeply into the spirit of laws. Society rests upon force; force must be respected as the august foundation of all societies.

"Now justice is the administration of force. M. le Président Bourriche knows that Officer 64 is *une parcelle du Prince*, that is, an integral part in the machinery of government. The Government resides and acts in each of its officers. To impair the authority of Officer 64 is to weaken the State. To eat a single artichoke leaf is to eat the artichoke, as the theologian Bossuet says in his sublime language here and there in his *Politique Tirée de l'Ecriture Sainte.*

"All the swords of the State are turned in the same direction. To oppose some swords to others is to overthrow the Republic. That is why Crainquebille, the accused, was justly sentenced on the testimony of Officer 64 to a fortnight in prison and to a fine of fifty francs. I can almost hear the Presiding Judge himself setting forth the high and noble principles which inspired his sentence. I seem to hear Monsieur le Président Bourriche saying:

"'I judged this person according to the evidence of Officer 64 because Officer 64 is the emanation of public force. To establish my wisdom, you have but to imagine my acting otherwise. You will see at once that it would have been absurd. For were I to pass sentences unfavorable to the powers of force, these sentences would never be carried out. Notice, gentlemen, that judges are obeyed only when they have force on their side. Without the police, a judge would be nothing but a futile dreamer. I would be hurting my own cause were I to acknowledge that a policeman might be in error.

"'Besides, the very genius of the law is opposed to such a sentence. To disarm the strong and to arm the weak would be to change the social order which I am committed by oath to preserve. Justice is the sanction of injustices which have become established. Was justice ever found opposed to conquerors and contrary to usurpers? Let an unlawful power rise, justice has but to recognize it and it becomes lawful. Form is everything: the only thing that distinguishes crime from innocence is the thickness of a sheet of paper bearing seals and a ribbon.

"'It was for you, Crainquebille, to prove the stronger. If, after shouting *"Mort aux Vaches!"* you had proclaimed yourself emperor, dictator, President of the Republic or even alderman, I assure you I would not have condemned you to a fortnight in prison and a fine of fifty francs. I would have acquitted you and you would have gone scot-free. You may take my word for it!'

"So, doubtless, would M. le Président Bourriche have spoken, for his is a judicial mind and he knows what a magistrate owes society. He defends its principles with order and regularity. Justice is social. Only antisocial persons would champion a justice that was human and subject to compassion. Justice is administered according to fixed rules and not with regard to the feelings of human hearts and the clarity of human minds.

"Above all, do not ask justice to be just; it need not be just precisely because it *is* justice. More, I dare say that the idea of a justice that were just can only have been born in the mind of some anarchist. It is true that Monsieur le Président Magnaud

pronounces equitable sentences, as in the Dreyfus Case. But what happens? They are swiftly appealed, reversed, and that is justice!

"The true judge weighs testimony according to the weight of the weapons behind it. That is what took place in the Crainquebille trial and in other even more famous cases."

Such were the arguments presented by Monsieur Jean Lermite, the etcher, as he walked up and down the famous Salle des Pas Perdus, that lobby called The Hall of Wasted Steps, where lawyers and others walk up and down, chatting between cases.

Maître Joseph Aubarrée, a lawyer who knew the Palais de Justice and its Courts, scratched the tip of his nose and replied:

"If you care to hear my opinion, I don't think that Monsieur le Président Bourriche, our worthy Presiding Judge, ever rose to so lofty a metaphysical conception. To my way of thinking, admitting the testimony of Officer 64 as the expression of truth, he simply acted as he has always seen judges act. Imitation furnishes the clue to most human actions. By conforming to custom, a man can always pass for respectable. People are called righteous men when they do as others do."

V

Of Crainquebille's submission to the laws of the French republic

HAVING been led back to his cell, Crainquebille sat down on his chained stool, lost in astonishment and wonder. He himself was not quite sure whether or no his judges were mistaken. The Court had concealed its inherent weaknesses under the majesty of form. He could not possibly believe how he could be in the right as against magistrates whose reasoning he had not understood; he could not possibly conceive how anything might have gone wrong in so stately a ceremony. For, since he did not attend Mass or visit the President of the French Republic at the Elysée, he had never in all his life witnessed anything so

grandiose as a Police Court trial. He was fully aware that he had not cried *"Mort aux Vaches!"* Accordingly, to be sentenced to a fortnight in prison for *having* cried it seemed to him to be an august mystery, one of those Articles of Faith to which believers adhere without understanding them — an obscure, dazzling, adorable and terrible revelation.

This poor old man acknowledged himself guilty of having mystically offended Officer 64 much as a small boy, studying his Catechism, acknowledges himself guilty of Eve's sin. His sentence had taught him that he had cried *"Mort aux Vaches!"* Therefore he must have cried *"Mort aux Vaches!"* in some mysterious fashion, unknown to himself. He was transported into a supernatural world. His trial was his apocalypse.

If he had no very clear notion of his offense, his idea of his penalty was no clearer. His sentence appeared to him to be a solemn, ritual and superior thing, a dazzling thing which was beyond all understanding, which did not admit of discussion, and which was cause for neither self-gratulation nor self-pity. If in that moment he had seen Monsieur le Président Bourriche, the Presiding Judge, with a halo about his head and white wings on his shoulders, descending to him through the parting ceiling, he would not have been surprised at this new manifestation of judicial glory. He would have said:

"This is just another phase of my trial."

Next day, his lawyer came to see him.

"Well, my lad, you're not too badly off, eh? Cheer up, a fortnight is soon over. We haven't too much to complain about."

"As for that, I must say the gentlemen were very kind, very polite; not one oath, not a rude word. I wouldn't have thought it possible. And the '*Cipal* had white gloves on. You saw that, didn't you?"

"All in all, we did well to confess!"

"Maybe so. . . ."

"Crainquebille, I have a good piece of news for you. A charitable person, whom I interested in your plight, gave me the sum of fifty francs to be used to pay your fine."

"Well, when shall I get the fifty francs?"

"They will be paid into the office of the Clerk of the Court. You needn't worry about that."

"All right. Still, I thank that person very humbly!"

And Crainquebille, meditative, murmured:

"What's happening to me is surely strange . . . strange . . . ."

"Oh, come now, Crainquebille, don't exaggerate," the lawyer replied. "Your case isn't a rare one, far from it."

"Maybe you could tell me where they've stuck away my pushcart?" Crainquebille asked.

VI

Of Crainquebille at the bar of public opinion

After his release from prison, Crainquebille once again pushed his cart along the Rue Montmartre, calling: "Cabbages! Turnips! Carrots!" He was neither proud nor ashamed of the adventure that had befallen him. The memory of it was not painful. To his mind, it seemed to partake of the theatre, of travel and of dreams. He was especially happy to be trudging through the mud over the paved streets of the city and to see overhead the sky, rainy and dirty as the gutter, the loved sky of his city. He stopped at every corner for a drink. Then, untrammelled and joyful, he

47

spat into his hands, moistened his calloused palms, grasped the shafts of his pushcart and drove it forward. Ahead of him, flights of sparrows, as poor and abroad as early as himself to seek their livelihood on the streets, flew off in garlands before his familiar cry: "Cabbages! Turnips! Carrots!"

An old housewife, coming up, felt his celery, and then:

"What's happened to you, Père Crainquebille?" she asked. "I haven't seen you for at least three weeks. Have you been ill? You're a bit pale!"

"I'll tell you, Madame Mailloche, ma'ame. I've been playing the gentleman and living off my income!"

Nothing changed in his life except that he began to go to wineshops more often, because he imagined that it was a holiday and that he had met some charitable people. At night he would return to his garret, feeling rather gay. Stretched out on his pallet — his flop, he called it — he would draw over him the sacks which the corner chestnut-vendor had lent him and which served him as blankets, and he would ponder:

"Prison? Well, there's nothing wrong with prison; you have all you need there. Still, a man's better off at home."

His contentment was of short duration. He soon noticed that his customers gave him the cold shoulder.

"How about some fine celery, Madame Cointreau, ma'ame?"

"I need nothing."

"What do you mean, you need nothing? Do you live on air?"

And Madame Cointreau — "ma'ame" — without vouch-safing a reply returned haughtily into the large bakery over which she presided. It was the same with other shopkeepers and with *concierges,* that powerful class of superintendents who rule the destiny of Paris apartment houses. Not long since, they had thronged around his green and blooming push-cart; now they turned aloof from him. Reaching the *Cordon-nerie de l' Ange Gardien* — that shoemaker's establishment, *At the Sign of the Guardian Angel,* where his judiciary adventures had begun — he called:

"Madame Bayard, ma'ame, Madame Bayard, ma'ame, you owe me fifteen *sous* from last time."

But Madame Bayard, throning it over her counter, did not deign to turn her head.

The whole Rue Montmartre was aware that Père Crain-quebille was newly emerged from prison and the whole Rue Montmartre henceforth knew him no longer. Rumors of his sentence had reached even the adjacent Faubourg Montmartre and the tumultuous corner of the Rue Richer.

There, about noon, he espied Madame Laure, his kindly

and faithful customer, bent over the pushcart operated by his rival, young Martin. She was feeling a large cabbage. Her hair shone in the sunlight like threads of gold spun richly into abundant braids. And young Martin, a nobody, a *sale coco*, a dirty bum, stood there, his hand on his heart, swearing there were no finer wares than his. At this sight, Crainquebille's heart burst. Pushing his cart alongside of young Martin's:

"It's not fair of you to be unfaithful to me!" he said in a plaintive, broken voice.

Madame Laure, as she herself recognized, was no duchess. It was not in high society that she had formulated her ideas about Black Marias and clinks. But after all, a person in any station in life can remain decent, isn't it so? Everyone has his self-respect and no one likes to associate with a man who has just come out of prison. Her only answer, therefore, was to turn away as though she were sick at her stomach. The old pedlar, resenting the affront, howled:

"Get along with you, you whore!"

At this Madame Laure dropped her green cabbage and cried:

"*You* get along, you dirty jailbird! He's fresh out of prison and he starts insulting decent people."

Had Crainquebille retained his self-control, he would never have reproached Madame Laure with her professional status.

He knew only too well that people cannot govern their fates or choose their professions, and that there are good people in every walk of life. He had always tactfully ignored what

might occur in the homes of his lady customers: and he despised no one. But he was beyond himself. Three times in succession he called Madame Laure a harlot, a dead cat and a bitch.

A group of idlers gathered round Madame Laure and Crainquebille as they continued exchanging further insults quite as
serious as the first. Indeed, they would have exhausted the
lexicon of vituperation but for the sudden appearance of a
policeman whose silence and immobility made them as silent
and immobile as himself. They separated. But this scene put
the finishing touches to Crainquebille's disgrace in the eyes of
the Faubourg Montmartre and the Rue Richer.

VII

Of the immediate consequences

THE old man shambled off, mumbling: "She's a bitch and a whore. And there's no whore more whorish than that one, God help us!"

But in the depths of his heart, that was not what he held against her. He did not scorn her for being what she was. Rather he respected her for it, knowing her to be thrifty and decent. In the old days, they had enjoyed chatting together. She used to tell him about her parents who lived in the country. And they both decided that they would some day have a little garden and raise poultry. She was a good customer too. But to see her buying cabbages from young Martin, a nobody and a dirty bum, cut Crainquebille to the quick; and when he saw her pretending to despise him, it made him see red, and, well, there it was!

The worst of it was that she was not the only woman to treat him like a mangy cur. Everyone shunned him nowadays. Just like Madame Laure, others — Madame Cointreau of the bakery, and Madame Bayard of *L'Ange Gardien* — scorned and repulsed him. Yes, the whole of society was against him!

What! Just because a man had been put away for a fortnight, he was not even good enough now to sell leeks! Was that just? Was it good sense to make a decent man die of starvation because he had had differences with the cops? If he couldn't sell his vegetables any longer then he might just as well lie down and die.

Like a poorly doctored wine, he turned sour. After having had words with Madame Laure, he now had words with everybody. On the slightest provocation or on none, he would tell his customers what he thought of them, and without mincing his words, I can assure you. If they handled his vegetables too long, he would call them skinflints and deadbrokes; and at the wineshop, too, he would bawl out his pals. His friend the chestnut-vendor now cut him dead, qualifying that damned Père Crainquebille as a regular porcupine. Nor could this be denied, for Crainquebille had grown quarrelsome, foul-mouthed and noisy. This was, of course, because, finding society

imperfect, he lacked the facility with which a Professor of the School of Moral and Political Sciences expresses his ideas on the vices of the system and on the reforms necessary. Also, his ideas were not organized with precision, order and moderation.

Misfortune was making him unjust. He would take revenge upon those who wished him no ill and sometimes upon people weaker than he. Once he slapped Alphonse, the wine-seller's little son, because Alphonse asked him whether he had really ever been in the clink.

He boxed his ears hard, crying:

"You dirty little brat! It's your father should be in the clink instead of getting rich by selling people poison!"

Neither that deed nor those words did him honor. As the chestnut-vendor justly observed: one should not strike a child nor reproach him with a father who was not of his choosing.

Crainquebille now took to drink. The less money he earned, the more brandy he drank. Formerly economical and sober, he himself now wondered at the change in him.

"I was never a high liver!" he said. "Truth is, a man's wits probably don't improve with age."

Sometimes he would pass stern judgment on his misconduct and idleness.

"Poor old Crainquebille, you're no good for anything now save to bend your elbow!"

Sometimes, in self-deception, he persuaded himself that he drank of necessity:

"I've got to have a nip now and then, you know. It gives me strength and freshens me up. Certain it is that there's something inside me burning my guts, and the only thing I know to quench it is drink!"

Often he happened to miss the morning sale at the Halles so that he was forced to buy damaged vegetables on credit. Once, feeling weak in the legs and weary at heart, he left his pushcart in its shed and spent the whole blessed day hanging around Madame Rose's tripe-stall or in front of the wineshops near the Halles.

In the evening, sitting on a basket, he meditated and became conscious of his decline. He recalled his early strength and his ancient labors . . . his extreme fatigues but his happy profits . . . the numberless days he spent, active and serene . . . the floor of the Halles which he paced at night until it was time to buy his daily stock . . . the vegetables he picked up by the armful and arranged artistically on his pushcart . . . the burning hot cup of black coffee he wolfed at one gulp from the counter at Mère Theodule's . . . the shafts he gripped so stoutly . . . his cry, strident as a cock's crowing, rending the morning air . . . his progress through the crowded streets . . . his whole, innocent, rough life, the life of human packhorse . . . the full half-century during which, on his rolling stall, he had brought to city folk, exhausted with anxiety and vigils, the cool harvest of country vegetable gardens....

Shaking his head, he sighed:

"No, I'm not the man I was! I'm done for! You can do just so much and no more. Then I've never been the same since my run-in with the law. No, I'm not the man I was, and that's the truth of it."

In a word, he was demoralized. A man in that state might as well be flat on his back and unable to rise. All the passers-by trample him underfoot.

VIII
Of the ultimate consequences

Poverty came, black pov-
erty. The old pedlar, who used formerly to come back from
the Faubourg Montmartre, his bag crammed with five-franc

pieces, had not a single *sou* now. It was winter. Evicted from his garret, he slept under pushcarts in a stall. It had been raining steadily for twenty-four hours; the gutters were overflowing and the shed was flooded.

Crouching on his pushcart over the polluted waters, with spiders, rats and famished cats for only company, he was meditating in the darkness. Having eaten nothing all day, and deprived now of the chestnut-vendor's sacks to cover him, he recalled the fortnight during which the Government had supplied him with bed and board. He envied the fate of prisoners who suffered neither cold nor hunger. And, suddenly, an idea occurred to him: "Now I know the trick, why not use it?"

He rose and went out into the street. It was a little after eleven. The night was chill and dark. A drizzling mist was falling, colder and more penetrating than rain. Passers-by, few and far between, hugged the walls of houses for such shelter as the roofs afforded.

Crainquebille passed the Eglise Saint-Eustache, a church hard by the Halles, and turned into the Rue Montmartre. The street was deserted. A policeman stood rooted on the sidewalk by the apse of the church under a lamp-post; a fine rain fell all around, reddish in the gaslight. It spattered the policeman's hood; he looked chilled to the marrow. But either because he

preferred the light to the darkness or because he was tired of patrolling, he stayed under his candelabrum, perhaps making of it a friend, a companion. Its flickering flame was his only resource in the loneliness of the night.

In his cold immobility, he did not seem quite human. The reflection of his boots on the wet pavement, which looked like a lake, prolonged his shadow downwards and lent him, from afar, the aspect of some amphibious monster, rising from the waters. Closer at hand, as he stood there hooded and armed, he suggested at once a monk and a warrior. The crude features of his face, emphasized under the shadow of his hood, were placid and melancholy. He wore a thick, short, grey mustache. He was an old cop, a man of about forty.

Crainquebille stole up to him softly, and, in a feeble, hesitant voice, said: "*Mort aux Vaches!*"

Then he awaited the effect of these consecrated words. But they had no effect whatever. The officer remained motionless and mute, his arms folded under his short cloak. Out of eyes wide open and glistening in the shadows, he gazed at Crainquebille with an expression of sorrow, watchfulness and scorn.

Astonished but still retaining a vestige of resolution, Crainquebille stammered:

"I said: '*Mort aux Vaches!*'"

There was a long silence. The reddish, fine rain kept falling. Icy darkness reigned. Finally the policeman spoke:

"You shouldn't talk like that . . . It's certain sure that's no way to talk . . . A man of your age should know better . . . . Move on!"

"Why don't you arrest me?" Crainquebille demanded.

"If we had to run in all the drunkards that talk as they shouldn't, we'd never have time for anything else. Besides, what good would it do?"

IX

Of Crainquebille and the darkness

OVERWHELMED by such magnificent disdain, Crainquebille stood there for a long time, dazed and silent, his feet in the gutter. Before going away, he tried to explain:

"It isn't to you yourself I said '*Mort aux Vaches!*' I didn't mean it for you any more than for the next man. It was just an idea I had."

With an austere gentleness, the officer replied:

"Whether it's an idea or anything else, that's no way to talk. When a man does his duty and goes through a lot of hardships, he shouldn't be insulted with senseless words. I tell you again: Move on!"

Crainquebille, with head bowed and arms limp at his sides, plunged into the rain and the darkness.

THIS BOOK WAS PLANNED BY GEORGE MACY; THE PRINTING

OF THE TEXT WAS DONE BY THE NATIONAL PROCESS COMPANY

FROM TYPE COMPOSED AT THE AKERMAN-STANDARD PRESS

IN PROVIDENCE; THE ILLUSTRATIONS WERE REPRODUCED

BY THE PHOTOGRAVURE AND COLOR COMPANY FROM PLATES

PREPARED BY GEORGES DUVAL IN PARIS